For Kåre Roger.

We love you. We miss you.

BLOOMSBURY CHILDREN'S BOOKS
Bloomsbury Publishing Inc., part of Bloomsbury Publishing Plc
1385 Broadway, New York, NY 10018

BLOOMSBURY, BLOOMSBURY CHILDREN'S BOOKS, and the Diana logo
are trademarks of Bloomsbury Publishing Plc

First published in Great Britain as *Leaves* in September 2021 by Bloomsbury Publishing Plc
Published in the United States of America in June 2022
by Bloomsbury Children's Books

Library of Congress Cataloging-in-Publication Data
available upon request
ISBN 978-1-5476-0899-7 (hardcover) • ISBN 978-1-5476-0900-0 (e-book)
ISBN 978-1-5476-0901-7 (e-PDF)

Book design by Goldy Broad
Typeset in Old Claude LP
Printed and bound in China by Leo Paper Products, Heshan, Guangdong
2 4 6 8 10 9 7 5 3 1

My Love Will Never Leave You

STEPHEN HOGTUN

BLOOMSBURY
CHILDREN'S BOOKS
NEW YORK LONDON OXFORD NEW DELHI SYDNEY

He had watched over and cared for her from a seedling.

When she was bare and small, he had pointed her to the sky,
helped her branches grow true and strong.

He had kept her sheltered
from the storms,

shaded from the
scorching sun.

And, supported by his love,
she grew
and grew.

One morning, as they sat and watched the sun rise together, she asked about the leaves that covered his branches—all heart-shaped, fresh, and green.

"These are memories of the life I've led," he told her.

"I've tried to let go of all the bad ones and hold on to all the good ones that have grown."

She asked if she would ever have any leaves like that of her own.

He took her hand.

"Come with me and I will show you—
it's time for you to see and learn."

They walked upon the hills
and sat by gently flowing streams.

They watched birds dance in the sky
and let them find refuge in their branches.

They skipped through meadows,
surrounded by the fragrance of
the flowers now in bloom.

He taught her all he knew—
how to be gentle and kind
to those around you.

How to provide shelter
and to share.

How to be strong against the wind
but flexible enough
to bend.

Soon *she* had leaves too, all heart-shaped, fresh, and green.

"Feel the sun on your face . . . ," he told her.
"And the breeze blowing through your leaves.
Although your limbs and twigs may twist and turn,
with patience all will heal and grow.

But, above all, don't forget to
sometimes let things be . . .

to STOP and enjoy the view."

They walked above a peaceful valley,
and she saw some of his leaves had fallen.

"Do not worry," he told her. "Some moments you must let go.
But remember to keep the dear ones near—
for good memories will shelter you from the storm.
And the great ones will keep you warm."

But as time passed,

and the weather grew colder,

she noticed he had fewer leaves . . .

and then fewer.

She asked him why.

"I have taught you everything I know.
Soon you must travel this path without me.
We cannot stop the seasons.
We have to let it be so.

It's nearly time for me to rest,
for I have no more leaves to grow."

As he spoke, his leaves turned so light, so bright, and so full of color.
They glowed warmly, all yellow, orange, and red.

Because when a tree has no more leaves to grow, those they held the closest,
and loved the longest, turn bright with life before they start to fall.

"Come with me," he said. "To feel the breeze rustle
through our leaves is what a tree must do."

So they ran one last time through the hills,
far away to a place they had
never traveled before.

Together, they stopped above the view.

"This last leaf is my first memory of you," he told her.
"All heart-shaped, special, and golden.
I will always be with you.

Each time the wind blows, in your leaves
is where you'll find me . . .

But for now,
it’s time . . .

and I must go.”

The winter closed in.

Alone and afraid, she didn’t know
how to get back.

But as the storm howled around her,
twisting, turning circles in the cold,
she heard a gentle whisper in her leaves.

She stood strong and still until
the wind dropped.

Ahead of her . . .

A shining trail
of his leaves
in the snow.

Bright memories
of them together.

Bright memories
keeping her safe and warm.

Bright memories . . .

Guiding her home.